PUBLICATIONS

FICTION:

Current Wisdom

Reckless

The Flying Horse

POETRY:

Argument for Mercy

The Journey of Lost Things

APPLE iBOOK:

Reversing Paradise

A LAKE IN HEAVEN

A LAKE IN HEAVEN

J C WATSON

VIOLETCLAIRE PRESS ❧ CALIFORNIA

INTRODUCTION

Emmy enters the Aspirancy at the age of 13 completely taken with her desire to become a saint. Aspirancies flourished from approximately the 1930s in this country until the mid-60s. They served various religious orders of Roman Catholic Sisters by culling young girls most often taught in the lower grades by these same sisters, girls who had become mildly brainwashed by them. Emmy's life at home is violent, chaotic, and unpredictable. On her initial visit to the convent the contrast of seeming respite makes a deep and abiding impression as it is meant to.

Our protagonist enters religious life into this Aspirancy, of The Sisters of the Suffering Savior, a kind of prep school for would be nuns, just as the modernization of the Church has begun, mid-twentieth century, to an order of sisters that derives from Hungarian and French nuns that had historically been Cloistered. The Cloistered Order is separate from the external world and monastic; its members practice a strict Holy Rule of silence, fasting, and mortification of various types.

Many of Emmy's superiors and teachers were in flight from the Hungarian Revolution of 1956 and the years of persecution previous, and were loathed and appalled at Pius XII's requests in 1955, to modernize. They kept on, if not in practice, then certainly in intention, with their original Rule.

Research for the religious institution of The Aspirancy is scant indeed. Personal experience, therefore, will have to serve here for what has been repressed in the history of Roman Catholic Religious Orders in the United States. What this author has discovered in attempting to learn that history is that Pope Pius the XII wrote that the punitive nature of these aspirancies was not in the best interests of the young applicants to religious life. The Holy Father added that girls ages 13 to 18 required the support of their families and the social nature of friendship and that for proper development girls needed experience in the external world before commitment to life as a mature nun. In this same letter to the "Body of Christ," as the entire of the Roman Catholic Church is known, he called for a return to modern dress for the sisters and asked that "their sixteenth century garb" be placed aside. All these requests of Pius XII's were fulfilled eventually but gradually, and not without considerable resentment on the part of many orders of nuns in the states.

Aspirancies differed greatly from one order of nuns to the next. They most often were attached to boarding schools as had been Emmy's high school originally, but in the case of the Sisters of the Suffering Savior, a fictionalized name for this order still in existence today, the school was merely a day school for girls in the area.

Emmy's aspirancy followed closely the Rule of its parent order, which meant silence for most of the day except school hours and the hour of recreation from 7 until 8 each evening. Talking at meals was permitted at a sign from Sister Superior and at her whim. Contact with the aspirant's family was limited to one letter a week and one ten minute phone call which required reportage to her Superior. Friendships were discouraged for fear of intimacy developing between girls.

Another goal of these aspirancies was to rid the child of any egoistic habits by pointing out various behaviors, so that the child learned humility and her place in this new world.

Emmy's story occurs in a brief period of the Roman Catholic Church after which Aspirancies were further discouraged by the Second Vatican Council, which convened on October 11, 1962. After the Council, the existence of the Aspirancy rapidly waned.

But our protagonist has no knowledge of a changing church. No radios, nor television, and no daily paper were permitted. The girls were owned wholly by the order they joined; they were encapsulated in silence, mortification of the spirit and the body, and denied as much as possible, human attachment.

How will Emmy fare in this environment? Will she become her *best self,* she asks?

This work is a memoir, but it is a fictionalized one, so that the privacy of those who appear here might be protected. The story is presented in a non-linear fashion except for the concluding chapters so as to mimic to the extent it may be possible, the manner in which memory arises from the subconscious to the conscious mind.

ISBN: 978-0615878478

Published by VIOLETCLAIRE PRESS, Mountain View, California, January, 2014.

BOOK DESIGN: JCWatson, William Watson

COVER PAINTING: Paul DeLaroche, *A Young Christian Martyr*

DEDICATION

For my sons, who in my youth could not be imagined, these young men who fell from the sky like shooting stars, whose light burns still illuminating my days and dark nights.

ACKNOWLEDGEMENTS

With unending gratitude to William Harold Watson whose geyser of energy and compelling focus made the dream of this book a physical reality. My dream, "A book in my hands . . . :" this book.

Enormous thanks to my readers for their valued observations and suggestions: Marylee McNeal and Mary Jeannine Murray, accomplished artists in their own right.

Darkness cannot drive out darkness;
only light can do that.

Martin Luther King, Jr.

We are not always right
about what saves us.

Bruce Weigl, What Saves Us

Job feels the rod,
Yet blesses God.

New England Primer, 1688

. . . **a**ny system of religion that has anything in it that shocks the mind of a child cannot be a true system.

John Paine, The Age of Reason

I don't believe in God, but I do believe in His saints.

Edith Wharton

A LAKE IN HEAVEN

ONE

THE VIGIL

October, 1962

Dark. The red tabernacle light. The tongue of it. The smells of Butchers' Wax and old pine. I am on the altar, the forbidden place. I know the crucifix hangs there with its huge Christ, whiter than pearl, the black blood in long tears from His head, blood, weeping from the lance wound, the nails incorrectly placed. Is that soft footstep Sister Bernard? *I am desecrating this place.*

The old nonsensical priest would have a start, but he is long asleep dreaming his dreams of pot roast and flowers. The pews creak of their own accord. The pines are wooing and scraping.

There is nowhere for me to go. Not home to my pregnant mother, grey haired, wiry with anger. To my father, lost in the basement sewing buttons on strangers' clothes. Because of my brother in Viet Nam and my sister due one month before my mother. Because of the sisters, the little girls, pulled from Catholic School for lack of money.

Eleven o'clock. In the Chapel on the convent side of the school. The Sacristy. *Is the altar a sacramental? No girl has ever knelt here. And what will happen to me, to my sainthood? I need this place for holiness. The world out there is full of easy sin and here sinning it is so difficult.*

Four girls are gone, just this past semester. Vanished. I expect to home. Lucy, already a saint, tumbling like a sack onto the basketball court.

Merika, Ellena, the other Emmy. We have been instructed in Monthly Meditation not to utter their names. There is a crack in my chest. Each night my heart beats to get out, to be done with it.

"God of the lost, God who Himself was abandoned, God of the suffering mother, God who like me, belongs to nothing, save me."

I am a tallish girl, sixteen, a waif my mother calls me. I have pale skin and disgusting freckles. I have lank dark hair and bushy eyebrows. I am altogether unfit for this world. I don't remember exactly when I started thinking I might be able to pry the pipes apart in the radiator and stick my head in.

I rise and feel my way out through the crooked wooden door, into the convent library, and through the metal fire door, into the day school. Up the wide terrazzo steps, through the metal door, and into the old convent where my bedroom, at the end of the hall, receives me.

TWO

THE PROMISE

Spring, 1953

When Emmy was seven and on the kneeler, receiving her First Communion, it had come to her, this solution, this way she would not have be like her mother. This way she would never have a baby inside her and no money in the bank. This way she would not have to wait in the dark for a man to come home. This way she could be buried alive because a small white bed was all she needed and her body was no good for being seen. She would be a nun. Not, somehow, like the nuns who taught Catechism, the towering, black swishing, bad toothed foreigners. But like the nun who came to church one Sunday to ask for help. The plump white gowned woman with the large silver heart on her chest instead of Jesus on the Cross. She'd said she was taking care of "Lost Girls." For Emmy it was a terrifying thought that girls could be lost. At the same time, it was lucky because those plump happy ladies would shelter you and you could learn to sew or write shorthand and never go home.

But Emmy knew she did not want to be a nun. She did not want to teach, and never, never would she want to be a nurse and see bleeding or dying people. She hated the kitchen, so she could not be a cook, and she found old people menacing and unreachable, so she would not be able to care for them. But by the time she will be nine or ten and in Catholic School, the nuns will begin to talk about the saints. Emmy will have Catherine get her a book from the bookmobile, The Lives of the Saints. She will begin to have a sense that time is running out. The Sisters of the Suffering Savior will be stopping by her desk, old Sister Mary Germaine especially. Until this time she will have been comfortably invisible gazing out the window, under scrutiny only during arithmetic flash cards when her eyes snapped open and her mind went dead as a fallen bird.

They will say, "The end of sixth grade, then pretty soon seventh, then eighth. What did she think God wanted her to do with her life?" But Emmy will not be able to imagine. The only knowledge she will possess is that she is supposed to be Perfect as her Heavenly Father is Perfect. She is not to Sin against the Ten Commandments. She is to abide by the Corporeal and Spiritual Works of Mercy. She is never to be Greedy or Lustful. She is to Turn the Other Cheek. What she will cling to is that the Meek Shall Inherit the Earth. Emmy never wanted anything of the earth, but being meek herself, will like the idea that she will get something without having to be a loudmouth like Joyce Haines who once liked her and invited her to her house in Burlington overnight, but has since changed her mind.

What Emmy will want desperately will be to dance, and perhaps to act and sing. Her Grandmother Wilson thinks her fine at these things and will offer to send her to The Children's Playhouse School, but her mother Berta will not allow it, will insist that Emmy would have to "bow down to Grandma Wilson for the rest of her days."

But at seven even before she knew any of this, when Emmy knelt to receive the host, she promised God the Father and the Son and the Holy

Ghost that she would be a nun. Before she'd even heard about the nuns who prayed all day and didn't speak. Before she'd learned that some nuns consider themselves Brides of Christ and get to wear thick golden rings. Because if she became a nun, she could become a Saint, and God would look on her with such tenderness that the darkness inside would fly out.

THREE

BOBBIE

January, 1961

We are looking everywhere for Bobbie. Sister Bernard allows us all to break the Silence, but we are too frightened to speak. The place we think she will be is in the basement behind the cooler, the oldest part of the convent, dug out long ago, the ceiling so low even the freshman girls have to stoop. We have no refrigerator. The cooler is what keeps things, but it isn't cool enough and the milk is often sour and the butter off. After we check the basement with the aid of two or three exposed light bulbs and a weak flashlight, peer under the candle making station and the cement washtubs, we open the huge, thick cooler door. Andi screams and we all cry out, but it is only butter, three feet high, bending slightly at the top.

It is stranger than strange going through the cavernous kitchen and dining rooms at night. Lots of us wear nightgowns made by Bobbie's mother. Up to the neck we look like Bobbie. In the school, the classrooms seem haunted as though ghostly girls sat at the connected desks. We hold on to each other's nightgowns; we are not allowed to touch each other's hands. The ferns look grey. The blackboards swallow the dark. We don't even think about outside, the gardens, the pigs and slop, the limping farm hand.

The terrazzo floors gleam with the wax we have laid down on our knees, glare from the great shiner that's pulled all of us every which way until we understood to let go. The presidents are dour, disapproving. Suddenly I realize that I love Bobbie and seeing her face in front of my mind makes my head ache. Sister Bernard unaccountably, warns us to be silent and directs that we will go into the convent and up into the attic. A shudder runs through me. The other girls look wild. I have only been there once to make a replica of the Library of Alexandria with the other Emmy. Our small troupe climbs the narrow stairs, bleached and concave with age. It is unheated and January. We are just back from Christmas and I feel the same old feelings. Sick about leaving my sisters, glad to have left home, feeling the arduousness of our lives, alone as I am ever likely to be.

There is no switch. Sister must go in and find her way to the hanging bulbs and their square black tabs. I hear what sounds like muffled swearing and some bumping of heavy furniture and then see finally, light. Inadvertently, the other Emmy and I hug and dig our heads into that space between our necks and shoulders.

Old steamer trunks are everywhere. The flooring is of broad boards, never stained. Some costumes hang from the rafters; they seem dead and worldly. The attic is endless. Magda gets the idea to look in the trunks and this takes us some time. Every time someone lifts a lid we gasp. All at once, Sister Bernard motions for us to stop and then again, for us to back up. We huddle. She opens a door in the eves that I did not know was there. We can see nothing when sister's arm shoots out, a white predatory bird, and pulls Bobbie, old fashioned flannel nightgown, face melted and soaked with tears. I have never seen anyone who had cried as much.

We are helpless. I know this is the end of something. Bobbie is a senior. Late this month she will become a postulant. Sister Bernard hugs her to herself and we look at each other astonished.

"We go to bed now," she commands. "We will be silent now. Everything is alright."

FOUR

THE SILENCE

September, 1959

When Emmy'd finally gone to the convent as an aspirant, she'd been thirteen. She had been shown her bed and dresser in the dormitory that had once been a library, a cavernous room with twenty foot high ceilings. Huge windows rose at the end of it that were to offer up stunning displays of electric storms. "Twelve little girls in two straight lines, the smallest of which was Madeline." The picture book popped into Emmy's head and remained there. Two rows of white metal beds, twenty, with white chenille spreads, twenty small wooden dressers for their underwear. The older girls kept one small prayer card and a crucifix in the fold at the rise of their pillows.

Each night, on the stool at the foot of their beds, they lay out their under things, shoes and socks on the floor below, blue school uniform on its hook to her right shoulder. She learned to dress in bed, balancing the blankets on her shoulders.

All this Emmy did in blind obedience; she had always been an obedient child. But what shocked her—there was so much she had not been told—was the silence. From a small cottage in a housing plan at the edge of farms and woods, a house filled with people, seven children and two parents, from a kitchen so small the refrigerator barely fit, noise was all she had ever known. Bathroom noises, kitchen noises, her father's workman clambering up the basement steps, the phone ringing endlessly, and the bickering, the yelling, teasing and always, very loud music.

There was silence observed in the dormitory, silence, of course in the classroom, silence in the dining room until Sister Bernard proclaimed "Praise be Jesus Christ," silence on the way to chapel, silence in study hall, and the Great Silence observed after 7:30 Recreation at 8:00 sharp. This, Emmy learned at her first monthly meeting, termed the Monthly Meditation, included "custody of the eyes." Sister Bernard trained her refrigerated gaze on the new girls. She seemed to have notes in a small black leather book and referred to them now and again.

"What we mean by silence is complete. It is possible to speak with the body in gesture and posture. We will not. It is possible to speak with the eyes, conveying an entire conversation in supposed silence; I have observed just such conversations among some of the girls. This will cease."

She felt the silence pressing against her eardrums. She constantly thought of things to say. And worst of all, the silence made friendship almost impossible. Already she loved Magda. She was a big girl, her bones, but she laughed so deeply and so hard, and despite the no touch rule, somehow knew when Emmy was having a bad day and would pat her shoulder. She was from Hungary, a refugee, and she had a riotous, difficult time with English. When she called Emmy's name in basketball, it was emMee!, emMee!

One afternoon when she was walking down the school hallway, Sister Bernard, called, "Emmeline!" Emmy stopped mid stride and whirled about. They were not to speak in the hallways. Sister's face came so near, she caught the odor of her afternoon tea.

"If you could see yourself walking; it's too jerky. Your head moves like a chicken's."

Here Sister paused to demonstrate,

"Yes, a chicken." A nun moves fluidly, her arms calmly at her sides, her neck upright and still."

Again a short demonstration, a kind of statue on wheels. Emmy was stunned. After Sister Bernard went on and disappeared into the convent side, she was paralyzed. Emmy was ninety pounds. Her knees stuck out, her elbows; her chin came to a witch's point. It would be impossible to move elegantly. And this in a girl who imagined she would dance if she had not been becoming a saint.

FIVE

VISITATION

September, 1962

This is one of the reasons I cannot go home. My mother is pregnant. She has grey hair she covers up with tint, but still, it is grey around the edges. Somehow my mother is pregnant because my sister is pregnant. Something wrong with her thermometer. I love my father, but now I hate him. I hate all men who make women pregnant. I hate the corset I laced my mother into in the morning. I hate the black rope veins in her legs, and the elastic, plastic looking stockings she wears that make her sweat like crazy in the summer time. I hate that my mother is so sad and so angry she cannot love me.

Today is visitation. No one will come for me but my mother, not the little girls, never my father. We have two hours, a long time and a short time. In the ten minute conversation (once a week we may talk by telephone to our families for ten minutes exactly) my mother has finally told me. She will have the baby in December, a Christmas baby like the Christ child. She tells me she is trying to be brave, to be like Jesus on the Cross. My mother has still not talked to my sister Catherine; she doesn't know where she is. This seems impossible to me who must report all that has been said to Sister Bernard—the pregnancy, my sister disappearing with her boyfriend, the bank calling about the house payment. This reporting is part of the thing called The Rule, but there were actually hundreds of rules within the Rule. No secrets. "We are open books to our Superiors. Our lives belong to Christ, now. Everything."

Berta is late; now we have ninety minutes. All the other girls have their visitors and I feel blue, anxious, orphaned. When she arrives, I am surprised to see that my mother looks only a little pregnant. She is all in black, a loose black shirt over a calf length black skirt. A kind of sad elegance. I am wearing my black aspirant's habit with the Peter Pan collar, starched stiff and steam pressed. We are dark women together in a hostile world; finally we have something in common.

From out of nowhere, from some door in the silent halls, Sister Bernard is manifested. From lips that seem sewn together she says tightly, motioning with her thin fingers, "Please, come this way."

I hold the door open for the two women, now three in black, and we slip into the convent. I, because all the nuns' bedroom doors are left open, can see the small rooms with their tiny beds, each with its collection of relics, rosaries, and prayer cards. I make up my mind to have nothing on my bed. I will remove the glow-in-the-dark rosary and the prayer to Saint Maria Goretti, child martyr who died with twenty four stab wounds (I think, as if one for each hour of the day) because she would not yield to a farm boy.

Glancing beyond me, Sister says that with my mother in "her situation" it would perhaps be better if we met in the nuns' parlor. I realize not one of the other girls has seen my mother. I say nothing; my mother says nothing, but studies the parlor's colonial oval rug for some time. I study the picture on the wall, a dark charcoal drawing of a woman in early 1900's dress seated at her dressing table, all the perfume bottles and creams in a line against the mirror. I see from just this distance that it is meant to resemble a skull; the mirror is the bony head, the back of the woman's head and her reflection are the eyes and the bottles and creams—the uneven teeth. I get up to read the title: Vanity.

Sister says she will come for us and she does, but late after everyone has slipped into study hall, upstairs near the dormitory.

SIX

MIND

October, 1962

The aspirant was obliged to reveal the exact moment one of them decided to leave. She was to come to Mother Superior and say that she did not have a vocation. Then she was supposed to pack up her trunk and leave in a flash. The other girls had all disappeared so silently. No one had ever seen a girl, her parents shuffling her into their station wagon, her things being stuffed into the rear of it. Emmy finally figured out that their parents had come in the night when she was asleep.

Emmy had known through her sophomore summer this last, after she'd gotten home and realized some of the aspirants had gone crazy. They had fallen over during basketball, or had screamed and run around in the middle of English class, or they had just stopped everything and lay on their beds. She thought somehow, all that summer that there was a wild thing growing inside of her. She had always been a little crazy. Given to dark storms that went on for days and fits of ecstasy when she was out of doors. But last school year when she'd grown into sticking pins into her hands so that she could suffer for the souls in Purgatory, that some might be set free; at that same time a dark busy cloud settled over her heart.

But Emmy could not tell them she was afraid of going crazy; there were several reasons for this. She didn't know any other way to become a saint. Her mother couldn't abide one more thing going wrong; she was certain, with Emmy at the convent, that Berta would go to heaven. And Emmy was sacrificing so that her brother would come back from Viet Nam. Besides, Emmy hated home. She hated home with everything inside of her. She hated the noise. She hated her mother's screaming. She hated her dad with his face in his hands at the dinner table. She hated not knowing where her sister was. She hated the bank calling.

Last summer she tried gently to open the door to her freedom. Emmy told her mother that she wanted to go to the dance with the youth group at St. Theodore's. Berta turned from the sink, violence on her face.

"Make up your mind, Emmeline! You want to be a nun or you do not! You can't have it both ways."

But Emmy wasn't thinking boys and girls. She was thinking, *dancing.*

Sister Bernard, one night, sent a postulant to Emmy with the message that she must come to her classroom. She was almost asleep. Ten o'clock. She sprang into her robe and slippers, and went out into the school hall, wide and cold, and descended the steps to where Sister was waiting, shimmering and dark by the giant fern Emmy daily watered and cleaned. *How can we be talking now, after The Silence? After everything she said?*

"Emmeline," Sister Bernard sat fully clothed at her desk with the lights up and bright.

"Sister Bernard."

"What do you think we are here for?"

"Why, (it was some kind of test) to become Sisters of the Savior."

"Not HERE, Emmeline—on this earth!"

Emmy was not certain that she knew. She studied the beige linoleum, its cream streaks, for some time. *What kind of person can think up such an ugly design?*

"Well," she began, "not really for ourselves . . . we are here to help save others. I mean our lives are not about our lives; they are about praying constantly for others and helping those less fortunate."

Silence. She glanced up in fear. Sister crooked her finger. "Step closer," she commanded. *Cold and heat.*

"I have something to tell you that you must never forget. You have a fine mind, Emmy, a great gift from God. You can serve us well with this light you have. You must not disappoint the Creator."

The nun spoke somberly, sadly, shaking her head slowly back and forth. A flush fired in Emmy's chest and roared up towards her cheeks; she was speechless, her eyes bugging open.

SEVEN

TESSIE AND LARK

December, 1962

We have two games. Basketball and Dodge Ball. I love basketball even though I dread breaking my glasses. I hate my black glasses with their swooped up points, Cats'-eyed they're called, but know there can be no new ones. Breaking them would mean sitting at the front of every classroom under each sister's nose, no staring out the window. It would mean squinting and misspelling things and not being able to recognize the girls I like in day school.

Dodge Ball is the game of madmen. Tessie is continually knocked over as am I. Tessie has my bones but is shorter. She has thick glasses just the opposite of mine—she can't see close—and they are huge. She always looks wise like an owl, but she isn't very smart. She doesn't dodge. She is Hungarian also, but was born here. Tessie loves "The Little Flower" for whom she has been named and has at least twenty different prayer cards to her on her bed. We are not allowed more than two things.

I think of Tessie as my Little Sister even though as a junior I've been assigned to Helen. Helen is supposed to come to me with her "adjustment problems." But she just passes me notes in the hall and I to her because there is no place or time for us to talk. Tessie's hair is black as midnight and except for her glasses, she looks exactly like Snow White. That's my nickname for her, Snowy. When we play Dodgeball, Annie and Magda get all fired up because I won't try to knock Tessie down. Recently, just as I was drifting off, Tessie knocked on my door (in our junior year we get to have our own rooms) and slipped in under the covers and buried her head in my neck, weeping as though it were the end of the world. I wanted to know what the problem was, but she said we couldn't talk; it was after the Silence.

I have a secret friend in Day School. I haven't confessed to the old priest; I haven't told my Superior. I consider this a venial sin and think it's okay to receive communion if I ask Jesus to forgive me each time. Her name is Lark, which can't be a saint's name, but maybe they used her middle name, which is Anna after the Mother of Mary, the one who had Mary in her old age. I shudder every time I think of being all bony and wrinkled and full of arthritis like my grandmother Rohrbach, and bearing down to have a child and how would your old flat breasts fill with milk?

At recess after lunch, Lark and I try to stand close to groups of girls, so it will not look as though we are talking alone together. Lark tells me she is Japanese American and I can't understand this because I know about the war. Her mother now lives in Hawaii and she's not sure where her father is, so even though technically, I have a father living with me, he is always working so we are both fatherless women. Lark is exotic. And her name is so perfect because her eyes fly up at the ends like the wings of a delicate bird. I am thin and she is thick, but in every other way we are alike. She didn't know when she passed me her poem in English that I was writing too, almost every night in my Spiritual Notebook in which I was supposed to be writing my spiritual thoughts and I did, but I have this urge to sing.

One time last spring, we were allowed one day with any Day Girl because the painters were coming. Of course I chose Lark; her older sister came and drove us to their apartment for the day. Somehow she and her sister Mary Lynn, not her real sister Lark told me, had been adopted by two very old spinster sisters who were foster mothers as well, but I could never have been prepared for what I saw. All the rooms were full of cribs, 5 or 7 to a room. The living room, what would have been the dining room, and one of the bedrooms. When we arrived the old sisters were having tea in the kitchen and nodded but made no move to ask me my name, nor tell me theirs. Several babies were crying and one was screaming, but their tea went on uninterrupted. Lark made no mention of any of this, just led the way to her bedroom, which was exactly the size of my parents' closet. The walls were cluttered with heroes and poems. It was the first time I had seen a black man on anyone's walls, three pictures of Martin Luther King. We lay on the striped seersucker bedspread and talked and read all afternoon. When it was time to go back for dinner, Lark drove with her sister and myself; she got out of the car and walked me to the metal doors that led downstairs to the kitchen and dining room. All at once we both started to cry, I'm not sure about what, then we hugged, just as the first snow of winter stung our cheeks, icy needles.

EIGHT

THE INTERVIEW

April, 1959

Before Emmy could come to the Aspirancy there had to be an interview. She went with her mother where they met with Sister Bernard who seemed simultaneously aloof and intense and with Mother Bridget, the principle who was tall and broad as a man; her face, Emmy was ashamed to have thought it, resembled a shiny ham, but Emmy liked her immediately. She had such a gentle, intelligent expression. She hadn't seemed concerned about why Emmy wanted to come. Even so, Emmy could not express to either of the nuns and certainly not to her mother that she wanted to become a saint. The convent was just the easiest way she could think of to become one. Already there had been some kissing in the back of movie theaters and Emmy could see how easy it was to get off track. She would later, and gradually, be told the rules. She seemed to be on trial before Sister Bernard, who asked her what she thought of leaving her family. Emmy closed her eyes a moment; she saw her mother's hands on either side of Emmy's head, felt her hair being pulled and her head rammed again and again into the dinette wall.

"It will be hard, especially—my little sisters . . ." her voice trailed off. Her three little sisters thought of her as their mother. She didn't know what would happen to them.

ırse, Jesus left Mary and Joseph to do .is Holy Father."

es, of course I understand," Emmy cast a sı.. glance at her mother, hatted and gloved, her mouth pursed. Emmy could see she was biting the inside of her cheek.

"It's just they're so little."

"But in time," Sister Bernard's eyes sparkled darkly, "they will understand and be proud. Perhaps even want to imitate you."

Emmy looked down. She was sick to her stomach. Finally, her mother spoke in a strained voice that Emmy had never heard before.

"But even though Emmeline will be here to become a nun, the Academy of the Suffering Savior is still a boarding school?"

"Well Mrs. Wilson, we used to take boarders but no longer." Sister Bernard looked confident and was it just a wee bit condescending?

"But the day girls," Her mother's face was blanched, her lipstick too red. "They pay a monthly fee, do they not? And the aspirants pay for their education—isn't that so?"

Sister Bernard raised her delicate eyebrows slightly; then a light came into her eyes. She lowered her voice to a confidential pitch.

"Mrs. Wilson, if I understand you, you must put all these fears about money behind you. We never let money stand in the way of a girl's vocation!"

Her mother stared at the nun hard and then looked away.

They toured the grounds. The old red brick buildings hunkered low. Old pines shushed and whistled. They made a visit to the a white cement statue of Mary as Our Lady of Fatima with the three shepherd children who had seen her, Lucia, Francesco, and Jacinta.

The aspirants were called down from study hall to meet her mother and herself, and in that moment, Emmy's heart was completely captivated. The girls were laughing, joyous and warm in their black loose dresses, black berets. Perhaps she too would be happy, innocent, needing nothing.

It was late when she and her mother got into the old yellow station wagon. As Emmy rolled her window down, Gregorian Chant rose from the chapel tucked into the pines. She stared at her mother and her mother back at her. Perhaps God was *truly* calling her.

NINE

VOICES

June, 1960

They were off that day for a picnic and all them were excited. It was the day before they would leave for the summer. Emmy had a minute with Magda as they descended into the windowless kitchen to pick up their baskets.

"I will miss you so much, emMee!" Magda stopped on the first landing. She touched Emmy's arm and when Emmy turned to look at her, she saw Magda was distraught, even panicked. Emmy had thought the older girls were always calm. All of a sudden, though Emmy bit her fingers, she could not stop herself from crying. The girls threw their arms around each other, but Emmy could say nothing because it was all wrong. She could not say, *I do not want to go home; I want to come with you to your parents who still look haggard from the war and the revolution. I want us to be girls together. Friends.* But they pulled up and stopped, then continued down the steps as if nothing had happened.

Sister Emille was the only one in the kitchen, just tucking the last bologna sandwich into its crinkly wax paper. She had the strangest eyes. They were dark stones in her all white habit, always seeing something, but nothing was in front of her. She would have been beautiful if she had been a man, but when Emmy looked at her she saw all rectangles. Head, one rectangle, shoulders to waist, another, then a rectangle on its side, waist to thighs, and then another final long rectangle to the floor. Sister Emille gave each of them a basket and it took all their strength to lug them up and outside where the others were waiting.

They were a small group, six freshies, four sophs, three juniors, and two seniors—-now postulants, who were allowed to come with the aspirants for the day, but it was doubtful what they could do with all those clothes on. The aspirants were allowed to wear their day clothes, but it was still a kind of uniform. Wide circle skirts (they were not allowed straight skirts in the convent), cotton blouses, but no belts—they were considered extra. They were a troupe and were allowed to talk all that day, but mostly they ran like kids across the old farm meadows toward the creek and the hills. The freshies had never been there. The woods they had to pass through to get to the meadows were dense, dark; there was a narrow path they followed with Sister Bernard up ahead, her walking stick pressing small holes, quick as a mountain goat. In the woods they grew silent, given over to their own thoughts. Emmy studied the way the light came down in shafts. She used to believe that light was God's grace; her mother said so. But she knew now God's grace was mostly unseen, floating about, available to give you courage. Emmy had never imagined how much courage every minute of life took. And so a voice inside her mind had begun to blink on and off, *Be strong Emmy. Keep your thoughts. Keep your thoughts, Emmy.* It was not a voice that had ever spoken before.

There were other voices. The voice of the mystic who loved suffering and guided her to burrow into it. The voice of the dancer who told her to tap dance alone in the bathroom. And then the voice of the poet who had Emmy scurrying just before lights out to hastily scratch down a few more stanzas of what was most real and secret in her heart.

Finally, they reached a sunny clearing and spread the old quilts on the ground. Here there was a pond, still and muddy with horrible water spiders opening and closing on its surface. But it was so hot and they'd walked for so long that Irene, one of the postulants, whispered to Sister Bernard who looked hard at the group, undecided. Irene stepped back.

"If anyone wants to swim in the pond, she may," Sister said at last.

Magda gave a whoop and ran, her strong legs pumping. Andi, the blond tiny freshman, always silent, followed her. Emmy closed her eyes to the spiders and the circling mosquitoes and plunged in, her skirts opening like an umbrella, the only one to go under completely.

TEN

BERTA

November, 1962

It's been sometime now that I think half the night away, fear filling up the dark so that it is something I can touch. Ever since returning from summer, I am afraid Sister Bernard can see into my brain, can read my shiftings, my unsettledness. Will see that I follow the Rule less and less. If I am caught kneeling in the deep dark of the altar, God forbid, I may be sent home immediately, a thorn in my mother's side instead of her crown in heaven.

But on a Sunday morning, a few days before Thanksgiving, Sister Bernard summons me to her side as the girls are silently withdrawing from the dining room, oldest to youngest.

"Emmeline," she takes both my hands in her fingertips which are freezing. "You must be strong, Emmeline."

A stone drops through my body.

"Your Uncle is coming to take you home. Your mother has been to the hospital, but they were not able to save the baby. We are giving you a special permission to go to her and help her through this difficult time. I have arranged with the teaching sisters to assemble your work for you to take. Go now and pack your things for one week; you will remain with your mother until after Thanksgiving. Your Uncle will be here in forty five minutes."

I squeeze Sister's fingertips, remembering too late that I must never touch a nun; they are sacramentals. To do so is a sin.

I pack my things in my pillowcase, taking my rosary and my Maria Goretti prayer card . . . I feel a swarm of feelings—a loud, solid relief that the baby is spared this life, relief for my mother, that it is over for her—that there will be no baby for whom she has to prop a bottle in the bassinet while she broils the meat cakes. Relief that the black veins in my mother's legs will go down and she can be normal. Relief for my father, bent over his desk, somehow like an animal yoked to a huge wagon. But anxiety too, how well is my mother after all this? Did she already love the baby? I did not. I was indifferent to it. I would have loved it like the rest when somebody placed it into my lap, but if it did not appear, more to the better for everyone.

* * *

Uncle Carl, my mother's brother knows me a little from times I stayed at my grandmother's house. He married late in life, since I've been at the convent. Everyone thought neither he nor his brother Tommy would ever marry. My happiest times were those I spent at my grandmother's following along with "the boys" on their trips to the store for my exacting grandmother.

"What did she say, Tommy, pork chops or pork loin?"

"Damned if I know. Just lean, baby, lean or she'll cut off our heads."

I bounced in the back seat amazed that anyone could take my grandmother lightly. I loved their swearing and said over and over in my mind, *Damned if I know, Catherine. Damned if I know.* They stopped for a streetcar. Five thirty, and the working girls descended, parading just in front of the Pontiac, their bright summer dresses whipping in a hot wind.

"Will ya look at that polka dot honey?" Carl nudged Tommy sharp. The boys' faces held wide grins. I stared straight ahead to Miss Polka Dot. Floating just an inch from the hood was a woman, rounded and proud in a blazing white and black polka dot sundress. Her hair was bleached, but still shiny, and she wore berry colored lipstick on her large mouth. Just when she reached dead center, the point of the hood, she turned and waved languorously. Carl tooted the horn just a little and Tommy blew her a kiss.

* * *

Uncle Carl places my pillowcase in the back and helps me into the front bench seat. For a moment I think that this is how a date would be, someone opening the door for me, checking, being solicitous. I am still in my black aspirant's dress and my Uncle seems impressed by this.

"I really admire what you're doing, you know that?"

"Why?"

"Well, a nun and everything. I couldn't do it!"

"Why not?"

"I'm not a good person. I'm mean, I'm selfish. I like to have a good time."

I think of telling him I might have to leave. How much more selfish than that could I be?

"Everyone likes to have a good time." I pat my uncle's arm resting on the ivory wheel.

"But don't you pray all the time and wash the windows and wax the floors, your mother tells me."

"Well," I feel like a fake. "We put on plays. I write plays. And we even have fashion shows. I made a Sari for the international one."

"So you sew, too?"

I laugh deeply. "No, that's why I was an Indian. You take seven yards of fabric and fold it a certain way and . . . you're dressed!"

Uncle Carl takes my things from the rear seat of the Pontiac and places them on the driveway. I get out slowly; he does not come in. As I pick up the pillowcase and my book bag, my mother opens the door and then the screen door. I notice that the storm door has not been put in place. Berta does not seem to notice I am here. She is looking out across the highway. A bus roars by. The wind takes the last leaves across the small hilly yard. My mother has stopped tinting her hair; I can see that it is salt and pepper, more salt than pepper. And then to my horror, I see that the baby has not left; my mother still holds it in her belly.

ELEVEN

THANKSGIVING

November, 1962

The first night home I bathe my little sisters, all three in the tub together, to conserve water. I am doing the same things I have always done. I soap their hair and pull it into peaks, placing the extra soap on their small fists, their ice cream cones. They giggle with glee. After the bath I wrap each one in turn in a towel, rolling the ends into a handle and fly each of them, supergirls around the living room. I then dress them in their thick, footed pajamas and towel dry their hair and brush it to the back of their heads. This is easy; they all have short hair for simplicity, two blonds and a dark haired girl. Rose and Angela, the blonds, just 16 months apart and Missy, the baby, black haired.

With Missy on my lap, Rose and Angela to my left and right, I read them The Night Before Christmas. For my amusement, I narrate with an English accent, but they squeal and wriggle in complaint so I must resort to American.

With Catherine gone, they are sleeping in our room now, the bunk beds having been moved up to the tiny attic bedroom. I tuck them in and we pray for God to bless our parents, our brothers and sister, the poor, the orphaned. My sisters will not let me go so I turn out the light and sit with them for a while. When they seem more settled, I rise and open the curtain to the hallway calling back, "Don't let the bedbugs bite!"

I descend the dark enclosed stairway carefully, feeling my way with my toes and hands—the light switch has never been fixed. My father is already in bed and my heart hurts a little over this. Like old times my mother and I take our seats on the couch in front of the window.

"Emmy," My mother looks pinched and pale—the baby sits low, low in her belly. I can't even think of a right question to ask.

"The baby's dead."

"But . . ."

"Sometimes it happens that the baby dies before it is born."

"But how will . . ."

"Emmy, I still have to have the baby."

"Dead?!"

Tears fill Berta's eyes for a moment, then follow a narrow jerky path to her chin. I stroke them away and also begin to cry. *To have a baby that is dead!*

"How long will it take?"

"I don't know." Berta takes a tissue, matted from her pocket and blows her nose. "The baby is due in two weeks."

Under the circumstances, I do not ask about Catherine. My mother says that it has been two months since she has heard from my brother James. She shows me the brass crucifix he has sent her from South Korea; it is still wrapped in dusty pink tissue paper.

For me, this time is a reprieve; my mother is too weak and sad to be critical and I am too busy with the girls and housework to think about anything. I sleep soundly. I even get some time with Suzy, my friend just up the highway. Somehow Suzy's family knows the baby has died, but they don't know my mother is still pregnant. When I relay this, they cannot hide their shock.

* * *

We have Thanksgiving with Grandmother Wilson. I am ecstatic. Grandma Wilson is now in the smallest apartment at the top of her old turn of the century house; she sleeps in a small pantry off the kitchen, though my Uncle Steven gets a nice bedroom with a down comforter on his bed. The apartment looks like a wind blew through it. Books are everywhere—the floors, chairs, books stacked up by Grandma's bed. And nick knacks, everywhere, strewn rather than placed. On my lap I hold the rose in its crystal ball plugged shut by a dark wooden base, press the cool round glass and peer up close at the petals of the giant flower with it's red exactly the color of blood.

TWELVE

THE BLESSING

February, 1961

I awaken in what must be the middle of the night. When I get out of bed and cross the cold wooden floor, I decide to get socks for my feet. Sitting in front of the bare window on the floor, pulling them on, I see that it is snowing across the wide convent lawns, a quiet snow, no wind, just an even blanket about six inches deep, glowing. The Mystic voice comes into my head, and I think I will go out there, walking. I will take off my socks and feel the snow under my feet. How many souls will fly up out of Purgatory? But then I think of Sister Bernard, in her long black cloak, coming upon me, shaking me—how she would comment in Monthly Meditation that some of the girls are suffering from pride and imagine themselves holy and above the Rule. How it is simple obedience, not great acts which please the Savior most. How all the girls will say to themselves, "I'm not like that." But I will be red with shame and some of them will notice and wonder what I have done.

* * *

We aspirants are included in the assembly for the Day Girls even though the discussion will be about dating and purity. Father McBride sports a rose on each cheek against his white, white skin. He has black wavy hair and doesn't seem exactly like a man or a priest. At the end of his talk about the spiritual nature of love, the sacredness of love, how human love is like the love of God the Father for God the Son, (I can't help wondering why the Holy Ghost is left out), the young priest takes questions. A tiny minute of a girl with dimples at the edges of her mouth and a smile that looks like a dare, Georgia Casoly, shoots up her hand.

"I'm confused; a lot of the girls are confused." She pans the students. "We don't know what is a sin and what is not. We think we can hold hands I guess, but are we allowed to kiss?"

Father is smooth as glass. His eyes display nothing. Georgia may as well have asked him if we are allowed to have dessert as well as dinner. He doesn't even pause.

"We must remember that the intentions and motives of our actions count even more than the actions themselves. Some kisses that are given in tenderness on the cheek or even lightly on the lips are not sinful if the intention is pure affection and not behavior of an animal nature." Father McBride's clean blue eyes sweep over the assembly. Mother Bridget stands at the back, like a guard, manlike, her hands crossed over each other. There seem to be no other questions, and I see most of the girls glancing out the windows or down at their laps. Deborah Mahoney, Georgia's best friend and opposite in every way except that they are the only two girls at school who wear lipstick, waves her large white arm. It is rumored that Deborah has been sent here to keep her out of trouble. Her eyebrows are squinched, but she looks clear, confrontative.

"But specifically. Then we are allowed to kiss on the lips—but what about French Kissing?"

A universal gasp is heard in the room under the glaring lights and suddenly the walls shrink; we are pressed upon one another. This time Father is not as quick. If eyes can wave then a large ripple moves across their calm blue.

"Your name is?"

This gives him some time. Deborah is still standing, bold as a flag. I am not sure what this is but my friends back home had already discussed "Frenching," and had agreed that it was a mortal sin.

"Deborah." She arches her left brow.

"But, Deborah, let's remember what it is about our behavior that most concerns our Heavenly Father. The behavior you ask about can never be construed as innocent or tender. It occurs when we transmute tenderness . . . when we yield to our lower nature. Since we are every day striving to resemble Jesus and his eternally pure mother we can see how such wantonness would cause them enormous grief."

Deborah's eyes glint. She shifts her left hip out and sits down slowly. Father McBride raises his hands in an ark; we understand he is going to bless us and we kneel except for Mother Innocence who is so ancient there is no figuring it. She leans behind Father on an old stool. She blesses herself the old way, with her rosary's huge crucifix, dotting her head, heart, left shoulder, right, finally bringing the corpus, with her wizened, shaking hands to her mouth.

THIRTEEN

THE FIELD

July, 1955

The meadow stretched out behind the bland red brick Methodist church on her left until it dropped sharply ending in the woods, Emmy's sanctuary. It was a steep hill but still, she could see far down to the tiny black winding road below, then across it and up another hill to a fenced meadow where the cows sat like small tan blocks. She loved the cows. Once, when they'd first moved to the country, before the church was built, she and Catherine had packed peanut butter and strawberry jelly sandwiches and had hiked with sticks to pull apart the raspberry vines and thistles all the way down the hill, across Old Town Highway and up to the farm to feed the cows the long grasses on the sister's side of the fence where they couldn't reach. This is how she had learned about electric fences. The cow slipped her head toward Emmy; she thrust a huge clump of juicy green grass through the wire, trying to avoid the barbs, but she was afraid—her hand jumped abruptly just as the great teeth chomped on the grass, at once connecting it with the barb and the zap of electricity.

* * *

She had been reading The Lives of the Saints. Now she was studying Saint Catherine of Sienna. The story revealed that in a meadow just like Emmy's, the great sky clouds had cleared one day, all at once, revealing The Host of Heaven. Emmy had imagined the scene: God the Father, God the Son, and The Holy Ghost, all the fathers of the church, Augustine, Paul—not Moses and Abraham; they were in Limbo still, for they were not baptized. But the Christian martyrs and the Children of the Crusades and Maria Goretti somewhere in the throng.

Emmy thought of this one day when she came into the meadow with her favorite stick and her black dancing tights on her head by way of "Indian Hair." The cumulous were bulging on flattened black bottoms. The wind came up and birds and sticks went flying. It was the height of July pressing with its wet air. Emmy's heart clenched. At once she wanted to be a normal girl to whom nothing miraculous would ever happen.

But at that very moment the clouds began to roll back furiously like ocean waves she had not seen, but had imagined, rolling over and parting like a heavy curtain. All at once, so faintly, shimmering, a city of glistening people appeared. At the front, God the Father on his throne looking white haired but not really old, Jesus beside him black haired, his black eyes ablaze, and the Holy Ghost, unlike the pictures she had seen—on fire, blue and orange like the flames on her mother's stove. They didn't seem to notice Emmy, but stared off into some far future. And all of them—the entire city, were weeping.

Emmy knelt, clutching her walking stick for some endless time. She would never know if she had really seen all this or had imagined it. It did not matter. All her life she would speak of it to no one. She would not have the life of some holy kid, full of reporters and doubtful, inquiring priests. She couldn't know if God were calling her, but did not think this was about herself. Somehow, even though she was barely nine, she thought that something terrible was making heaven weep. She thought of herself, playing and caring for her sisters, never thinking of some wider world, some way she could perhaps do something.

Without warning, the clouds sealed themselves and a fork of lightning shot into the field far across the way where the cows huddled together, heads bowed, shoulder to shoulder.

FOURTEEN

MEDITATION

December, 1962

I no longer sit in the front at Monthly Meditation. The younger girls do. We have a new girl who has arrived just after Thanksgiving. She is a big girl, large bones and stocky legs, a difficult Hungarian accent.

We sit for some time in silence, as is the custom; Sister Bernard's cool hands rest together on her desk like two flattened doves. Outside it is trying to snow, but the flakes dissolve into ice and then rain. I look down; we are to meditate, but I am still not certain what that is. I am supposed to think of the ways I can be a better aspirant, more pleasing to God. I am supposed to think of scenes from Jesus' life and see whether I am following His Way or not. I am supposed to face head on, the ways I am not following the Rule. But instead, I am wondering about the day I came into my room to prepare for bed and Helen swung out of my closet to frighten me. It was just as I was dipping my fingers into the small holy water font, a little boy on it in a strange, soft, pointed hat. I screamed; the font broke loose and crashed to the floor in a hundred shards. Immediately Sister Bernard entered my room and sent Helen to the dorm. It was after the Silence. The font lay at my feet and across the floor.

"What have you done? What have you done? Don't you realize," she said swooping up the largest piece and fanning it across my face, "that this is a

Hummel? Have you no idea when something has value? You will ask your parents for $25.00 to pay for this!"

My face stung. I thought something is wrong, but I didn't know what. Something about the font, I did not know what a Hummel was. But something is not the way God wants it, I thought, and some dark thing rolled over inside. I looked at Sister a long while feeling wild. She stared, her cheeks puffed and red. Then she whirled about and stomped out of the room.

We have our Spiritual Notebooks on the center of our desks. Each is crammed with holy cards and pieces of ribbon from gifts, though we are forbidden gifts. I write little prayers in my book, because I am beginning to think, when we meet in the dark chapel after dinner for rosary, *that it's too hard for our rote prayers to have any meaning. Isn't Mary getting weary of being told over and over in our drumming monotone that she is Holy? Why do we have to tell her this? I want to talk to God about what is in my heart. I want us to know each other. I know God has no interest in me, really. None-the-less, I believe He loves me and will listen out of politeness.* I told Him after the holy water font was broken that it was not my fault. That I would not ask my parents to pay for it. That if Sister Bernard asks them, I will tell them they will not pay, although I doubt they will listen to me.

I begin to pray. I tell God I cannot stay and I cannot go. I ask him just to get me to a place of peace where I can become a saint and all this Rule and praying in the dark will fade away and I can extend my arms as we do on First Saturday, kneeling on the floor of the chapel right in front of the Tabernacle and the Monstrance, and cry out to Him, because surely God has forgotten how we need Him to touch our lives.

"Praise be Jesus Christ," Sister nods towards us and we answer, "Now and forever, amen." She opens her leather book where her observations are listed. She says she wants to see better "Custody of the Eyes" during dinner before prayers. We are making faces about the food. We signal whether we are hungry and we are making funny faces to get each other to laugh. This will stop.

She adds that some of the girls are getting sloppy about bed making. We are to be meticulous. Every act no matter how common is at once sublime because it is being offered to God Himself.

But my mind wanders off to puzzle about the Trinity. I don't know to whom I'm praying to when I pray. In my mind I take all three and overlay them the way I saw cartoons being made on Disney. Otherwise, I feel I have to choose which manifestation I want to pray to, and I don't want to choose. I don't want to play favorites.

And then Sister pauses. The faintest flush fans her cheeks.

"There are some girls," ahem . . . "There are some girls who are simply not up to snuff with well . . . cleanliness. Though we each have but three minutes in the shower we can be efficient and not dream. There are girls amongst us who do not use deodorant. We must apply deodorant morning and night, no matter what was our habit before coming to the Sisters of the Savior. And . . . this is difficult, but some of us are not changing our sanitary napkins often enough. There is no excuse for this. Make certain your parents bring you sufficient quantities during visitation. I remind you that this is group living. We conclude Meditation with The Act of Contrition."

Emmy looks at the new girl, Mari, remembers her sitting on the radiator in recreation, her odors wafting throughout the room. Maybe in Hungary they don't know about such things.

FIFTEEN

VACATION

December, 1962

This time my father comes to fetch me for Christmas. It is all over for my mother. The baby has come. My father tells me that my mother is fine, that they had to take her to the hospital in an ambulance because they couldn't stop the blood.

We are in the van with the giant rug cleaning machines and the sponges and buckets. There is barely room for my pillowcase. A light snow falls and we have a long way to go, mostly over steep hills and roads that climb through the woods. I'm thinking I might never get home to see if my mother really is alive, to have Christmas, to see my sisters.

I listen as my father tells me about his new business. He has a crew, Al and Baby. I can't believe that's someone's name. They go into people's houses and clean their carpets and do something called pilating, something for the nap. He says it's good money, but that Al and Baby aren't so good. Lots of mornings he has to take a run by Dolly's Donuts and yell. Sometimes he catches them in the Old Town Tavern having fish sandwiches and beer. Or sometimes a woman claims a lamp or table was broken by the crew, but often it's just that she wants a new one and it's Al's and Baby's word against hers. And of course, my father has to give her one. He talks so softly. The window wipers shush. He laughs as he tells me these stories, but they just make me sad.

When we slide down the driveway, it is all a dream. The little yard is covered in the snow that looks like unwrapped cotton roll. The big colored lights are strung across the front of the house, and the little girls are in their pajamas jumping up and down just inside the picture window.

They rush me when I'm still outside on the stoop, and my dad says they miss me all the time. I get down on my knees and we are crying and laughing at the same time. I ask them is Santa going to come and they shout, "Yeah, yeah."

My mother calls in a weak voice from her bed and when I go to her, she weeps and holds me very tight. I am somehow surprised to see her. I sob into the front of my blue uniform and she says that she was almost gone and then at the last minute God called her back.

That night after everything has settled and my dad is snoring a little in the bedroom on the other side of the living room wall, my mother and I sit on the sofa in the dark in front of the large window. We don't say much but look out at the snow falling again in the streetlight opposite our house. We grab each others' shoulders when we see two rabbits, hopping slowly just in front of us, catching the light, in the curtain of shimmering, needling snow.

SIXTEEN

CHRISTMAS

December, 1962

On Christmas Eve while my sisters are down for their naps my mother and I raid the closets for their dolls. My mother's idea to remodel them seems like a hair-brained scheme. But once again we have no money and my mother hasn't been well so we are stuck. We spend a long time scrubbing their cheeks and limbs with a toothbrush and shampoo. We wash their hair and set it in doll sized plastic curlers, pink and blue. The day before, we had washed their clothes and ironed their dresses, a tedious task. After the scrubbing, we took their clean blankets and wrapped them carefully, placing each doll in a cardboard box, along with their new/old clothing. Each of the dolls has a new dress, shoes, and socks that we leave in their plastic boxes so that my sisters will have something to unwrap.

Tonight, after they have gone to sleep, we drag out the boxes and place them on their sides, dolls showcased with their new clothes inside. These boxes we place in front of our cardboard red brick fireplace, it's little aluminum fan whirring above the red nightlight bulb. We are satisfied, and I am happier than I have ever been. Just before I fall asleep, it comes to me that such happiness might be more plentiful than I had thought. What if I could feel something close to this more often than Christmas?

SEVENTEEN

LOOSENED

January, 1963

When I return after Christmas, one more junior girl has disappeared, simply not returned. Janey. No one really knew her; she had been so quiet. But, she is a neighbor of mine and I make a promise (another act against The Rule) to look her up come Easter and find out why she'd left.

Now there are only three juniors. In Monthly Meditation, Sister Bernard comes down hard on what all the aspirants feel is happening. The Rule is becoming loose at the corners. Two girls had been caught teaching each other to dance during what should have been their study hall. They were in the dorm, moving through the steps in complete silence, but sister had heard the odd shuffling from below.

Lark and I are now passionate about our writing and exchange poems almost daily in class. One day Mother Bridget, our English teacher, catches me editing one of Lark's poems when I am supposed to be reading Antigone. She plucked the poem from my desk, snorted, and asked me to leave the room. Somehow, I didn't fear Mother Bridget, mostly because we have something in common: we both love literature. I am her best student. But likely, she will tell Sister Bernard, and this tendency I am beginning to demonstrate, this individuating, will not be tolerated.

Otherwise, everything remains the same. Except in January, I get the job of cleaning the nuns' dining room in the basement. We are supposed to keep The Silence during our daily chores, but I never hear anyone around at that time. So, to amuse myself, I sing all the songs I know, the new folk music: Blowing in the Wind. The songs my parent's had brought me up on, In the Wee Small Hours of the Morning. Contemporary music: Barbara Streisand, Elvis Presley. I like to re-invent the songs in the huge echoey room. While I wet-dust the long black tables I sing. Mopping the khaki green linoleum, I sing Somewhere Over the Rainbow until my heart hurts.

One day the door opens to the dining room and Mother Bridget simply stands watching me. I stop mopping and face her preparing for the worst.

"With that voice, you give joy to God when you sing. Sing on Emmeline!" Then the tall, squarish nun vanishes.

I stand holding the long mop handle to my cheek trying to think. What was right? Being who you are or becoming something far, far better. And if you spend all your time becoming that far, far better thing is there any time left to become who you are? And which pleases God most, Mother Bridget's idea or Sister Bernard's? But mostly I feel the hand of kindness and am soothed.

Now suddenly, we are the older girls. The postulants have left for the Convent. Margee, Alice, and Magda. January 10th, they made their promises to God and were accepted by Mother Innocence. We aspirants were not allowed to witness the ceremony, because it possessed rituals only the nuns were permitted to see. The postulants still come to school of course, but with their new white bonnets and black habits, they seem to have jumped to some unreachable other side.

I miss Magda so badly; she had taken seriously the role that she had been assigned when I had arrived—that of Big Sister. Each day at recess she had spent as much time as was proper with me, asking about my family, if I needed any help with school, though I know Magda is struggling valiantly with this area of her aspirancy. She asked if I understood The Rule. To her, just before Christmas, I confided that I had certain doubts. I waited for the speech about leaving immediately, but it did not arrive. Magda bent her head and looked into my eyes, questioningly.

"God does not care if you become a nun or a coal miner, Emmy. He just asks you to live his way on whatever path you walk."

I squeezed Magda's hands hard. I was astonished; I had never heard this before.

After my talk with Magda, I begin to worry less. That is about being a nun. I could be a saint through any path, but I only half believe this. And if I am not a nun, then what? Praying in the dark on the altar, I beg God for a vision, not of the saints but a clear strong picture instead of the black emptiness. Dark on Dark.

* * *

Once again, when I am just about asleep, Magda stands over me, placing her hand on my shoulder.

"Emmy dear, Sister Bernard would like to speak with you."

"Where?"

"In her classroom."

I struggle up and Magda, looking like her old self without her bonnet, helps me into my robe and slippers. I stare at her, and she back at me.

"It's alright, Emmy."

The older girl walks me part of the way to the school building, gives me a small push and disappears.

Sister stares straight ahead as I enter the classroom, her fingers on either side of her nose as if thinking. I stand at her desk, awaiting acknowledgment. Gradually, so slowly, sister turns her elegant head towards mine.

"Emmeline, do you remember when I spoke with you about your mind, how you had a gift? "

I nod. Now sister's face is full upon me.

"Well, I was wrong. I was very wrong. You are dumb. I don't want you to ever forget this. You are very dumb. Do you understand?"

I am hit. I can barely stand. She nods again.

"You may go, Emmeline."

Before I turn away, I see at last the true color of Sister Bernard's eyes, silver. *Snake*, my mind offers, *snake*.

EIGHTEEN

GIANTS IN THE EARTH

August, 1957

Emmy awakened to hear her parents. She crawled across the floor to the heat vent feeling her way so as not to awaken Catherine. She was wearing her pants and summer undershirt for it was smacking hot, even in the middle of the night. Before they'd climbed to the attic bedroom, her mother had washed all of them down outside in their underwear under the icy cold hose water. Emmy had her mother press the hose deep into her hair for it was so much easier to fall asleep with a frozen head.

She opened the heat vent. It creaked and she looked towards Catherine, but she was not stirring. Most of the conversation was loud, but mumbled. Yet in the end, Emmy made out perfectly what her father was saying.

"It's not worth it. I just want to take the car and go over a bridge."

A few seconds later the front door opened, then banged shut. The station wagon on the driveway started up and she heard her father roar down the highway.

In the morning she raced down the stairs, still in her underwear to the station wagon; he was there on the front seat, fallen over like something folded.

* * *

August, and Emmie had begun to wish for school, not passionately, just a little. The sunlight was beginning to grow sad; it dipped. The saving grace of August had always been the fireflies. She and Catherine took their mayonnaise jar and poked holes in the lid with a fork and went out into the fields behind their house at dusk. They were going to make a firefly lamp. Emmy peeked a look at Catherine. Her cream skin and her tan freckles, her penny colored hair. Emmy had never seen a more beautiful girl.

On the spot, she wished she were beautiful. She had crooked teeth with a permanent brown spot on a front one that the doctor had proclaimed a fever stain. She was too thin. Her brother and sister laughed at her and called her bird stomach and snatched food from her plate while she simply stared.

By August most of the hated mosquitoes had been burned off and Emmy and Catherine wore shorts in the long grasses. The fireflies were pitifully easy to catch, and the sisters were greedy. Soon they had their lamp, perhaps thirteen fireflies in all, glowing green intermittently in the jar. Just as they began to screw on the lid, Catherine dropped the jar, snatched one more, turned it over on its back and wedged out the glowing part and put it on Emmy's ring finger.

"There, a firefly ring!"

Emmy was enchanted, then revolted and shook the dying belly from her hand.

That night in bed she thought of her mother, huge with her pregnancy. They already had a baby. Emmy wondered what they would do with two babies. She wanted to ask Catherine, but she wouldn't allow Emmy to talk to her while she was reading, so Emmy pulled up the sheet and sank into sleep.

* * *

Her parents weren't talking during dinner. Another customer said Emmy's father ruined his suit. Emmy poked at the canned grey peas and the grey broiled pork chops, at the applesauce, painfully sweet. She realized that everyone was sweating, and even though her father was cutting his chop in his shorts and undershirt, he answered the front door, which could be reached from his seat at the head of the table. Greg Rutter, 7, Charlie's friend, rolled in through the open door and stood up, eyes round and laughing.

Charlie was a mystery kid. The forth one in the family, born four years after Emmy, he had recently spent much of his time unsmiling since his best friend had been run over on Quincy Hill after sprinting from between two parked cars. They'd said a mass for him; Emmy was allowed to leave class and stand at the back of the gym they used for a church. The church was overfull and the song that Emmy knew only as a Christmas Hymn, "Oh, Come, Oh, Come, Emmanuel, and Ransom Captive Israel" was sung by the entire congregation as they brought in the little white box that held Robbie. Five days before, Emmy had come up to the attic bedrooms to see Charlie rolling around his bedroom floor, making animal sounds she had never heard, her mother trying to catch him so she could rock him on the creaky bed.

*   *   *

Eleven year old Emmy and ten year old Suzy attended what they waited for yearly, and for the first time without their parents: the summer festival at Saint Theodore's. They'd saved their quarters and dollars all summer—babysitting money. Night flowers hung in the air. They played Fishing and got nothing. They watched for a while as the young assistant pastor was dunked into the cold water tank by parishioners who threw balls at a latch that let go. They bought the red hot taffy apples and chewed them for a long while. Then cotton candy. All of a sudden a boy Suzy knew from the Methodist Church came up, and they walked around with him. His name was George; it seemed a strange name for a kid. Suzy giggled and didn't make sense; Emmy laughed too, but shyly. She thought that George was spoiling their night.

But soon, his parents came for him, then, Suzy's dad found them and took Suzy home. She watched Catherine and James for a while with a crowd of teenagers off by themselves. Emmy then searched for her dad and brother whom she found on an old blanket toward the back of the church field, but no James. How would he get home?

Now the moment she had been waiting for all year began. The rockets soared upwards and burst into showers of colored spangles again and again until the final display when some men down on the field, shadowed and silhouetted, lit the wooden and wire frames on the ground and sent what seemed like hundreds of fireworks into the smoky sky. Giants were rolling in the earth, she thought. Fabulous wild horses were pounding their hooves. Emmy felt the earth would break apart. The end of the Festival. The end of summer.

NINETEEN

A DOOR OPENED

August, 1960

Out of the blue, Suzy's mother called to ask if she could go to Cranberry Beach with them; Emmy had never been on a vacation except to go on the Greyhound with Grandma Wilson to visit her cousins in New York State when she had been twelve. She'd never forgotten that trip for two important reasons: for days afterward she felt the wheels beneath her. And she'd left her new dime store purchases on the bus. Candy pink lipstick, her first, and matching nail polish (though she had no nails) and rubber curlers that looked like small double flying saucers. Her babysitting money. She remembered the last moments on the bus, her Aunt Doris waving hello at the station. Whenever she thought about it, she walked herself backwards in her mind, back to the bus, the aisle, the seat—19B and bent down below the seat to pick up the crisp paper bag and in that moment, everything felt fine again.

Emmy ran up Jackson to Suzy's house, which was exactly like her own except with different furniture, big colonial furniture that shrunk the already small house even further. They jumped up and down together in Suzy's doorway, her blond Dutch boy flapping.

They left Friday afternoon. Two hours together in the back seat of Suzy's father's Chevrolet. They spent most of the time on their knees looking out the rear window, waving to all the truck drivers who waved back and honked in return. This made them collapse with laughter until Suzy's mother held her head (she got headaches that made her see colored stars and sometimes snakes) and yelled for them to "try another game." Counting out-of-town license plates was suggested, or counting cows, but there were too many.

Emmy wore her one new summer outfit, a denim sleeveless shirt and madras plaid Bermudas. She liked that the shirt made her green eyes blue, but thought her skin was too white. Suzy commented about their lack of a tan, after which the two girls traded phrases describing their condition that made them howl. Snow-girls, potato heads, ghost-bods.

When they got to the cottage she saw that it was a lot like her own house and was somehow disappointed. There was almost no furniture and only bare wooden floors. They jumped up and down again and ran upstairs to the little twin rooms. Emmy's room had a red chenille spread on the bed; that was her heart color.

They sat in the dark with the low hum of Mr. and Mrs. Harlow below. It was black dark and dead quiet. When they looked out the window, deep night stretched as far as they could see. Sitting on Emmy's bed, they brushed their hair one hundred times as they had been instructed by some teen magazine. Darts of light flew out and dissolved, falling stars.

* * *

In the morning they ran down to Cranberry Lake after Mr. Harlow served up banana pancakes for breakfast. Emmy thought this was the weirdest food she had ever eaten, but when she tasted it, she loved it and couldn't seem to stop eating.

It was only eight o'clock in the morning; the tiny beach was deserted. They were wearing their bathing suits but were wrapped in Mrs. Harlow's bathroom towels because the sun was still low and they were freezing. They took out their baby oil mixed with Mercurochrome and rubbed it on, preparing to roast all day. The lake was all tiny rivulets. Emmy had never seen a lake but had imagined large waves like in the movies. Early in the morning everything was bluish grey, the water, the sand, the trees, the sky.

"If you weren't going to be a nun, would you want to get married?" Suzy piped up out of the morning silence.

"Ugh. No. Never." Emmy was shaking her head, but no hair moved. Her mother had clipped it with the old bluish scissors into a Pixie. Suzy's hair was deliciously, fashionably straight. Emmy's was all dark squiggles and points, and it made her nose appear big and her eyes look monstrous.

"Why not?" Suzy looked incredulous.

"Because, I'd have to have babies. Because, I'd have to, you know, do all that stuff with a man that gives me the creeps."

"You don't think you'd like it?"

"Absolutely not. Kissing—that's all I'm ever going to do."

"My mother says you get used to it, and I can't imagine not having a baby. I mean what would you do?"

"I'd be a dancer. I'd go to New York and sing and dance and act."

"Why don't you?"

They looked at each other. Emmy could see that Suzy really wanted to know.

"I couldn't do that."

"Why not?"

"Because . . . I think what we're supposed to do is help people."

"Couldn't you help other dancers?"

Emmy looked out over the water; it was becoming a pale lemon color. She pulled at her hair; maybe pulling would make it grow. But a tiny match had just been struck at the back of her brain. She could feel the small heat; she could see the orange flicker.

* * *

On their last night, they went to Coney Island. Not the real one, a kind of a baby Coney Island. Mr. Harlow gave them his watch and some money and told them to meet him by the carousel at nine. The park was on the other side of the lake and the lights from all the rides danced on the water. Emmy was dizzy. She wanted to stay at Cranberry Beach for the rest of her life. They made their way from the parking lot of the tiny lake and stopped at the Ferris Wheel, which Suzy begged Emmy to go on, and she thought she could until she looked to where the cars plunged down, and she could feel her stomach sink and her head swim. A tall boy with hair as pale as Suzy's, in a bright white shirt, walked up with his hands in his back pockets and said,

"Hey, Blondie, I'll take you on if your friend doesn't mind."

He had identical dimples, each side of his broad smile, and Suzy looked at Emmy who shrugged, then she ran off with him. Emmy watched for a while until she got dizzy and had to sit down right there on the cement.

"Hey, you feel alright?" She looked up into the lights and neon and saw that a slender young man speaking with a slight Southern accent was peering down at her.

"Oh, I . . ." She was blushing. She could feel the tomatoes bursting on her cheeks. He reached out his long arm to her, but she didn't understand what he wanted. Then Emmy laughed, and he pulled her up. She felt his hand and realized he was missing its middle finger, and a shiver ran through her. Greensboro, North Carolina was where he was from; Emmy hadn't any idea where that was, but just then Suzy and *Blondboy* came staggering from the Ferris wheel. The boys shook hands. The boy with Suzy was Rick. The tall boy said his name was Clayton. They talked for a while but soon were looking around and down when Rick asked, not them, only Suzy, if she had been on the Jack Rabbit and she laughed and rolled her eyes and said it made her sick, but Rick would not let up and soon Suzy looked at Emmy imploringly once again, and once again, Emmy shrugged and off they ran together.

Emmy sighed and Clayton asked, "What's wrong?" She told him, "I'm going back to school and won't see Suzy for months." She was grateful he didn't ask her what kind of school, but only suggested that they walk down by the water where they could look back on the park.

When they got to the little boardwalk, she was astonished at the brightness of the lights bouncing on the lake, and though she was walking, she felt floaty. When they looked back at the rides, their shapes and colors burned into her brain. When Clayton bent to kiss her, a force inside Emmy's stomach pulled her away, but her head and neck rose despite her. She felt the delicate hairs above his mouth, noticed the scent of tobacco. She thought of the word swoon. *Swoon.*

Emmy didn't have Mr. Harlow's watch and let out running when she found at the refreshment stand, that it was exactly nine. But when she got to the carousel Mr. Harlow, who was very heavy, was mopping his damp face despite the coolness of the evening, was looking round and round. Suzy was nowhere nearby, and he asked where she was. Emmy said she had stopped in at the bathroom, that Suzy said she should come ahead to tell him. But he was never-the-less worried and walked to a park bench, placed one foot on the seat and hoisted himself awkwardly to scan in every direction. But all of a sudden she heard, "Emmy, Emmy." She turned to see Suzy running, her hair mussed, her cheeks glowing. As Mr. Harlow stepped down carefully, the bench shook; then he trotted towards Suzy. Emmy would have laughed if he hadn't looked so serious; he grabbed Suzy and hugged her hard.

"I told you not to walk around the park alone," he huffed.

But Suzy laughed and leaned her head back, her body swallowed up as it was, in his arms.

"When a girl's gotta go, she's gotta go!" Suzy sang.

*   *   *

In the black of her room, Emmy awakened to a stillness she'd never heard, not even at The Savior's. She knew something had awakened her, but she placed the pillow over her head and tried not to think. Suddenly, she saw an image of Clayton, heard his drawl, smelled the tobacco. There was a rushing in her body that started at her forehead and poured through like water. Except for Spin the Bottle in seventh grade and once in the movies, she had never been kissed. And not like that. Thin lip skin to let the heat out, softness to let her mouth dip into his, the feeling of strength in his arms. The way they'd fit like a puzzle. She'd grown five years in one night. Emmy knew she would not sleep. A door had been opened, and on the other side was another door. What was inside finally?

TWENTY

ONE OF A GROUP

March, 1963

I am kneeling alone on the gleaming pine boards of the Chapel with the bright lights above the altar beaming towards the monstrance in which the host is centered behind glass, glowing big as a hand. Its golden spikes radiate outward from the white disk like small contiguous swords. *They would be hot if I touched them.* We are not to use the kneeler. The floor below the altar and directly opposite the tabernacle is where I am—my arms stretched out, it is hoped for the whole hour, until another girl comes to relieve me. I am the one o'clock. It's been long enough that my knees are keening, but I am certain God is pleased so much that He may have allowed perhaps two souls to fly from purgatory. My brother may be getting on a plane for home right this minute.

Pictures of the lunch just eaten move behind my eyes and of me eating my lunch. I don't want to think about that; I must meditate. I must let the winds of grace move through me as God wills it.

I did not know what it was. Something mixed up. Relish. Maybe mayonnaise. I thought I recognized some of what was in the ice-cream scoop of material on the whitish lettuce leaf. Cautiously, I placed the first forkful on my tongue. Knobby, cubey. What? Hot dogs! From lunch on Thursday. The leftovers. Hot dogs, cubed in mayonnaise. With relish. I could not press my tongue to the roof of my mouth. I could only let each forkful pass along, washed down with the not cold enough milk. One, two, three. My throat was fighting back, my stomach had put the no crossing lever down. Ding. Ding. Ding. But somehow it went in. Four, five.

I've starched my collar too heavily. The pique drags on my neck. My stockings sag. My garter belt sags. My hips are too narrow to keep it up. I think of Maria Goretti, her last moments. Nothing compared to that. My glasses are missing their right earpiece so the room is askew. Things fuzz out of focus in my right peripheral field. I do not feel like a saint. But I understand that this is the beginning. I can say I am not a saint and God will not worry that I am putting on airs, asking too much of Him. He can't look my way; I don't want Him too. Only a little bit. He has to bring home the soldiers and feed the hungry. He has to hand down judgment a million times a day as many people are dying, even at just this moment, all over the world. He has to decide if they will dwell in His House of Many Mansions or Perish in the Flames. Why do they say "perish" when we don't die but feel the flames day after day, the ones that don't consume? That mysterious fire. If it wasn't for the pain, it sounded so boring, standing around burning.

With my right eye blurry, I thought just for a moment that the Host might be emerging from behind its round glass door. Perhaps it will come to hover over my head and tell me something I need to know. "Go, Emmy. I will keep you safe. Stay, Emmy, nothing can get you in here. No baby in your stomach. No banks, no arguments, nor doors slamming." I shut my eyes hard and say, *whatever He wants I will do.* When I open them the host is moving in a huge circle toward the crucifix, blocking out the suffering face. For a half moment, it rocks right there, then moves down and back into place.

* * *

It's night. I start to cough; I can't stop. My old iron bed rattles furiously. The wind is up and the pine branches scrape like thick fingernails. That big old branch looks like a witch's hand shaking her fingers. I know I am wrong. I have doubts but don't go. And I wonder again if the radiator can kill me. If I could get my head in there, but Magda says, "What do you mean, what makes it go? The water, emMee. You are crazy. The water makes it go."

I can't go to chapel. The nuns in the convent might hear me hacking. My diaphragm is sore. I am falling. I puff up my pillow and sit up, but then hang over it and cough till tears roll down my face, and the stuff from my nose pours over my open mouth. I am falling into something. I can feel the hands from some crowd below trying to get their fingers on my toes.

Then my old white door opens; Sister Bernard slinks through like a black ghost. She is fully dressed in the middle of the night and brings a cold washcloth, and something steaming in a glass cup. She says nothing, probably because it is The Silence, and only wipes my face and combs my hair with her long fingers. She tucks my blanket, beneath my chin, hands me the cup and motions for me to drink.

This is strange. Tea in the middle of the night, but I do as she instructs and after a few sips, the muscles in my chest begin to relax. I taste something like berries and see in my one light on the bed stand that my tea is red like cranberry juice. She leaves me to drink, and after I am finished, I place the cup on the stand and collapse until morning.

* * *

We march in a single line down the dirt road to the new Chapel. Soon there will be a whole new Convent. Birds skip through the dawn fog, but they do not chirp. Sister Bernard leads the way in her long black cloak that dances just above the mud. She rolls the black beads that look like carpenter bees through her fingers, her hands gloved in the type that have finger holes so you can do fine work and still keep warm.

I don't like the new chapel. It's too big. My father calls this feeling anti-claustrophobia. We don't need a chapel. We already have one. We need nothing new. All this newness and prettiness. We are supposed to turn away from *things*, to have nothing. Can basking in the light from the blue and pink glass of the windows bring us any closer to God?

We sit in strict rows, we aspirants at the rear with Sister Bernard sitting behind us to monitor behaviors. In the row in front of us, the postulants sit, then the novices, then the junior nuns, and finally the vowed nuns in front, according to age. Everything in the community is hierarchical, and I suppose this makes things simple, certain decisions simple. I don't believe God sees things that way, like who is the best, and who should sit in the front, and who in the back in heaven. But the nuns have already told us that the married will reside on the left hand of God and the celibate on the right. But I know God doesn't have hands or even a body, so how will people know where to go?

When it comes time for the Consecration, Novice Immaculata, who towers above me, who towers above everyone, blots out the old priest's head, his hands, the host. This is my favorite moment at mass when somehow, in a way that nobody understands, Jesus jumps back into the big white host that symbolizes the bread at the Last Supper and then also into all the little hosts that we will receive. I mean he comes right here, although, I am told he's always here, but I guess not his body. I have learned he is always inside of me so I don't understand why he has to come again, but I like it. It's like marriage, this coming together, but holy. His body inside my body. But what happens when the host dissolves, because all matter I take into my body dissolves—that's the nature of digestion. Or is this blasphemy? We don't digest God, surely. I move, ever so slightly to the left, away from the mountain shadow of Immaculata. I can see now, but just as I bow my head and touch my fist to my chest, I begin to cough again. And I know these coughs; they will fill the ears of the praying nuns, they will bang against the ivory walls and off the windows. All of that will occur thirty seconds from now.

I genuflect and leave so that I may cough outside and away from the building. Through the doors and out into the chilly dawn. When I can hold my eyes open, I see the slices of snow left from the last storm, see the sun—peach, behind the blue grey clouds. I see the pigs at slop, the limping farmhand. I understand that the world is entirely indifferent to me, to my coughing, to my falling, even to the host. It goes on despite all our prayers, flaunting its ordinariness.

A rough pull on my shoulder and I see it is Sister Bernard, and my fear makes me stop coughing immediately.

"Who do you think you are, leaving mass and at the consecration? You don't leave mass. And why are you not kneeling in formation, why do you not line up with Novice Immaculata? You must walk to the school alone now, and as you do, you must meditate on being One of the Group, not **One**—One of the Group."

TWENTY ONE

BLUE

May, 1955

Landscaping had been a luxury Emmy's family could not afford. An Indian Toby Tree grew huge and old at the top right of the tiny cup of front yard that bordered Jackson Highway, an old bus and truck run. Fine black grit clung to the screens of their house and inside on the furniture. The single flora they possessed at 255 was a tall Lilac Bush. Despite the soot and cars wrecking and occasionally falling into their yard, it thrived. Each May it bloomed its pale violet bounty. Berta cut boughs from the bush which never balked and brought them in for their makeshift May Altar. Usually it was Catherine's and Emmy's dressing table fitted with a blue taffeta skirt, hammered to the top edge with silver tacks. Blue for Mary. May was dedicated to the humble Mother of Christ, God, Jesus, Our Lord—whichever title might be utilized.

Emmy and Catherine stuffed pots and vases with those lilacs and violets from the woods. It was Berta's hope that Catherine, James, Emmy, Charlie, not Rose, for she was just a baby, would kneel on the landing of the stairs that led to the attic bedrooms each evening to say the Rosary in order to bring an end to Communism.

But it was Emmy alone who knelt there with the landing's one bare bulb hanging from its frayed cord, as she slipped through her fingers the cool pearly beads that she had received for her first

Communion. In the semi-quiet of after dinner—the pots and pans and the dishes being washed by Catherine and her mother, her father watching the news on the television with it's one staring green eye below the screen, her brothers romping in the long field down over the hill behind their house, and her little sister with her toys and balls in the living room. Sweet island in a violent sea. She prayed then, not for the end of Communism, but for her mother, pregnant again, five months, barely showing. There would be a baby in September. Emmy had sat on the basement steps just last Wednesday listening to her mother crying to Father Murphy. They didn't have enough money to eat, she'd said. Emmy remembered her mother cutting Charlie's pork chop in half so her father could have a little more.

"Hey," Charlie cried when Berta served him half of a chop, broiled and dry, "Where's the rest?" He was five and already tanned from playing outdoors. His hair was nearly white from the sun and sheared at the barber shop to last a long time.

"Your father needs a little more, Charlie." Berta was firm, Charlie's face, red with disbelief.

Emmy wondered why Father Murphy had said nothing. Her mother had been sobbing and blowing her nose in loud honks. But after he went away, Emmy brought the fifty dollars he'd left on the ironing board, and Berta cried all over again. Emmy prayed for her mother because she was pregnant—but what after all, what did Mary know about such things, she who had birthed only one child and her husband with a good job? But Emmy prayed also for her mother because at St. Theodore's they were taught to pray for their enemies as part of their study of the fifth commandment, Thou Shalt Not Kill. If you prayed for the ones who hurt you or might hurt you, God might give them grace enough to stop, and there would be more peace in the world. Her mother was not, strictly speaking, her enemy. But she had hurt her. Emmy stopped at the first Our Father and felt with her left hand, the back of her head; it still throbbed. It had happened when she'd yelled that she *had* washed the kitchen floor, she had even used Clorox on it. Had her mother even looked at it? Emmy wanted to know. Last night she had been setting the table for dinner, yelling this into the kitchen where her mother was chopping green peppers for chili, when she heard the clatter of her mother's paring knife into the enamel sink and in a bright flash, her mother pinning her between the chairs and the wall, pulling at her hair and pounding Emmy's head over and over against the pictureless wall till she'd sunk down beneath the chairs out of Berta's reach.

Finished with her prayers, Emmy came down the stairs to the kitchen and stood drying the dishes in the dusk dark room. She read the plaque over the sink; it always made her smile. "Lord of all pots and pans and things, since I've not time to be a saint by doing lovely things and watching late with thee, make me a saint by getting meals and washing up the plates . . ."

Drying and placing the shining glasses in the white metal cabinet to her right, she faced the church calendar and there, noticed the strangest picture of Mary she had ever seen. Her blue veil had slipped to her shoulders, her dark brown hair fell in thick waves, and her head was thrown back in laughter as she reached for the baby her aunt was placing in her upturned olive toned arms.

TWENTY TWO

THANKSGIVING

November, 1956

She'd finally finished helping her mother and sister with Thanksgiving dinner. The table was set and Emmy's dad had gone for Grandma Wilson. So she slipped out the door, calling over her shoulder—"I'll go for the centerpiece!" The day was raw, monochrome. She thought of black and white movies, her grandmother's stereoscope. Wind poked, icy, into the holes of her unmated gloves.

Emmy made straightaway for the meadow and woods behind The New Faith, the Methodist Church at the top of Jackson Highway. Passing the red brick building she wondered what Methodist meant. She knew method of course, a way of doing something, a procedure. What is their method, a method for what? All she had been taught about Protestant religions was that they were heretical. They were protests against the Catholic Church, and since her church relied on an Ex Cathedra policy—a direct line from God of his will here on earth—she knew that Protestantism was false. But she thought the people well meaning. It just seemed so boring. Once, in the summer when she had been weaving green sticks into the cluster of baby trees to make a type of Tee-pee, Emmy had to use a bathroom. She tried the door on the basement of the church; it opened easily. After she went in, she realized this was the place for Sunday school. Classrooms, desks—a bible on every one. She'd always wanted to read the bible, all the stories, but they were not allowed. Father Heinz said they were not to read the Bible for fear they might interpret it, and that they must not do. They did not have the education to understand the Holy Book. Priests did and would interpret it for them on Sundays.

Except for the bibles, the rooms were dreary. Emmy was used to crucifixes, statues, paintings—one in particular of Christ with magic eyes. Sister Eileen instructed her students to walk around the classroom and check back at Christ; she said that His eyes would follow them. They did and it was disturbing. They were to be reminded that He is ever watchful. Sometimes as she fell asleep, she imagined that picture just inside the classroom in the dark, the eyes moving back and forth, up and down searching for us, for our actions, seeing into us, our bad thoughts.

She was wearing James' cap with the furry ear covers snapped tightly beneath her chin which made the wind quieter than it really was. But it was quiet in the fields and she could feel the brown weeds of summer beneath her feet, their lacing of frost.

Emmy stopped short at the place where the meadow sloped gently to the woods. Queen Ann's lace and Milkweed with their wispy stuffings half out, looked odd, looked silver. A lemony light cut in behind the plants illuminating them as she approached. She couldn't move. They made a whirring in the wind. She sat down where the dried plants were taller than she was. She was inside them, inside the ice forest. The Queen Anns looked like frozen doilies, the Milkweed—wizards in the snow. It hurt behind her eyes; her head ached, but all at once the ice beneath her had become water and had seeped into her corduroy pants, through their flannel lining.

Emmy stood then and removed from her pocket the old blue-black barber shears she had taken in secret from the hallway closet. She cut a bunch with difficulty because the scissors were blunt with age and use, whispering, "I'm sorry," to something, something all around her. She then gently placed the frozen stems into a Kroger's bag, along with some long raspberry vines, yelping a little from their thorns. From her Tee-pee she also retrieved some long slender, very twisted branches that she knew her mother would not like, but which she imagined twining through the straight stems. Her centerpiece—right in the middle of the table for a little while, before the turkey was brought in.

TWENTY THREE

PRIDE

April, 1963

This Lent, my junior year, I sacrifice thinking. Sister Bernard has told me that my mind wraps around everything. Thus, I am constantly distracted from my spiritual path. And after all, my spiritual path has nothing to do with my thoughts, nor even with myself, but only with the honor and glory of God. About this I am horribly confused because I think that all the triumphs of God through Mankind have arisen from thoughts. Architecture and philosophy, science, surely. But then Martin Luther had thought himself into a bad place indeed and took half of Europe with him, so maybe certain kinds of thinking were evil. But how to know when and what? It will be easier to obey my Superior than to allow the dark shadow of thought to lie across my mind.

But a week into my experiment, I am having a difficult time indeed. I take to humming in my head whenever a thought pops up. Today, for example, all day I have been wondering why God likes men more than he does women. I long to be a priest. What is it to be a nun, really? A Bride of Christ, but not the one who stands for Christ himself, not the one who makes bread into God Incarnate. I want to wear the vestments with their shining white and gleaming gold. I want to reach into the very heart of human beings and lift the weight of their suffering. As it is, I will probably teach; I will never walk on the altar, nor open the tabernacle.

I have guessed that since Eve came second from Adam's rib, that my kind will always remain second. That we will never live in a house and have a cook and play golf on Sundays. But more confusion because it was Mary who gave birth to Christ, a woman, and where would Jesus be without her—the Catholic Church, Christianity? In answer to these questions, I hum.

I write at night in my Spiritual Notebook, but try not to think, to merely report on the events of the day. But why do I write about my day when I know already what has transpired?

When this time Sister Bernard calls me for one of her late night inquiries, she asks,

"Emmeline, what are you giving up for Lent?" Her grey eyes are the usual cold fires. This does not seem to be a real question, but a way to discover that I have been too lost in my daydreams to think about Lent.

"I'm giving up thinking."

A slight gathering of blood in Sister's cheek. A flick of light across her eyes.

"I see. How is that accomplished?"

"Mostly, I hum in my brain when I want to think."

Sister's gaze is steady, but at last falters. She looks down at her desk and picks up and releases her silver pen several times.

"Perhaps you have too many thoughts, Emmeline."

"I'm realizing that my greatest pleasure is thinking and that this is the perfect sacrifice. Besides . . ." Emmy blushes from her neck to her temples. "I understood as Lent came around that it's a sin of pride for me."

Sister Bernard clears her voice. The sound seems far away.

"How is that, Emmy?" There is something in Sister's eyes, and then she looks towards the calendar at the back of the classroom.

"Well," I am talking to myself, really, “when I try to understand things . . . like today I've been trying to understand why God likes men more than women."

At this Sister Bernard’s head lurches towards mine.

“I realized that I was feeling wise all of a sudden, as if I could figure out just about anything."

“Pride.” Sister says quietly.

"Yes. So, really I am sacrificing my pride. I am practicing not yielding to human ego."

Sister taps her pen on the blotter for a long while. I yawn. I am dead tired.

"Now, one doesn't want to become proud of not being proud does one?"

I am afraid. Another trap.

"No." I look down. The cream streaks in the beige linoleum wave like a snakes. I rock without meaning to.

"Emmy?"

"Oh." Would I faint? I place my hands on the old oak desk.

Once, I had fainted when I was twelve and the doctor, with my father in the examining room, moved his stethoscope closer and closer to my heart and into my bra cup stuffed with tissues.

TWENTY FOUR

PRACTICE

December, 1959

It was not until her first vacation that Emmy found she was going to lose her grammar school friends. Thanksgiving: the eight freshman had returned home with their unshaven legs and their classics to read.

When she talked to Toni and Roberta they yelled at her for not writing. She was quiet, still. She could hear their words over the phone, but they had no meaning.

"I wrote you guys, I wrote once a week and you never wrote to me at all."

Roberta was incredulous. "What? We both wrote to you every week for the first two months and nothing."

It hadn't made sense. What was the disconnection?

* * *

Back at the Savior's, in early December, Emmy pulled Magda's coat sleeve at recreation after lunch. They stood as if watching the Day Girls at dodge ball.

"My friends said that they never got my letters. Any of them. That's dozens."

"Hmm" Magda looked away toward the fenced garden in the distance. The day was bitter and Emmy had forgotten her gloves.

"And they said they wrote to me and I never got a one of them. Not a one."

Magda looked alarmed, her black eyes huge like a Gypsy's.

"emMee, didn't you know? They take them."

"Take them . . . ?" She thought, who? why?

"It's the way. It's the Rule. If anything in your letters is too revealing about the Savior's or if anything in their letters is too worldly, then Poof!, Gone!"

Whereas before Thanksgiving she had had two lives, after the holiday, she had but one. Roberta and Toni gave up. She gave up writing too.

One Sunday afternoon before Monthly Meditation, as she was writing to her mother, Sister Bernard appeared suddenly at her desk.

"Yes, sister?" Emmy looked up. Sister's face, pale onion skin.

"Look at your penmanship."

Emmy's heart turned heavy as she looked down. She herself had never liked the loops and circles of her writing and was disgusted that sometimes the letters slanted forward and sometimes backward.

Sister pointed a sharp nail onto Emmy's plain white paper.

"This must be changed. I want you to write more gracefully. The writing of nuns expresses femininity and the ability to yield."

She placed a lined paper filled with the alphabet, small and capitol letters, written in her own hand on top of Emmy's letter. The characters resembled fallen blue daisies.

"Practice the letters until your own closely match these. You may put away your letter to your mother—and by the way, what kind of a daughter does not write to her father as well? You must practice and every Sunday during Correspondence until it is time for Meditation."

* * *

It was Magda's birthday. The freshies decided for their skit to speak English in the way Magda did, with words like emMee and THANK-you. And Sister BERNard and Kolache for bread. This was Andi's idea and Emmy had been twitchy about it. But Magda laughed heartily and Emmy was pleased and relieved. The sophs made up a song with letters from Magda's name for the first word of each line like Misty, then, Always, then Grateful, then Dreamy, finally, Addled. It didn't rhyme which was very odd, but it did have Magda down to a "T." The juniors pantomimed Magda being a kitchen aide, buttering the toast endlessly; we all laughed until we cried, but no one more than Magda. The seniors, who seemed years and years beyond them, recited a long poem that detailed all of Magda's good traits. They all had tears in their eyes by the end.

After that, they were served a special chocolate cake, with icing that dripped all round and down the sides; it was Magda's mother's recipe and her favorite. Emmy loved it when they turned off the lights in the basement dining room and their faces glowed in the candlelight. She thought they should have candlelight every evening; it made her sad that they had any electric lights at all.

*   *   *

The school bathroom, which was Emmy's to clean for December, had like the hallways, terrazzo floors. When she cleaned on Fridays she wore her loafers so that she could dance a little. One toilet. One set of tapping. Another toilet, another set. Last Friday she had been dancing for her toilets and humming <u>Dancing in the Rain</u>, when the door poked open—Magda with her hair done up in huge brush rollers.

"emMee, you nut!" She rushed in before they could remember the Rule and Magda danced a minute beside her, ruffled her hair, and then was gone. She held on to the magazine pages they used to wrap their sanitary napkins, unable to place them in their baskets in the stalls, unable to move. A cold sheet of water ran down the inside of her body. *Lonely. Lonely.*

TWENTY FIVE

A LAKE IN HEAVEN

August, 1962

August, just before my junior year—I am getting ready to go back to The Savior's. My mother who is pregnant is ironing my father's white shirts. She has the ironing board set up in the living room and the western sun smokes on the other side of the beige, ropey curtains at the picture window. From the refrigerator, from a huge plastic bag, she takes the shirts starched and dampened with water from the coke bottle topped with the cork and metal sprinkler. On the dinette table an aluminum pitcher filled with melting ice and orange Kool-aid sits to quaff our thirst.

I am folding my flannel nightgowns, feeling hot just looking at them. Then my ironed bras. Magda showed me how. All at once I stop and hold one out from my face. Thirty-two AA. That's a baby size. I have the smallest chest in the convent. The nuns wear binders to make them flat; we saw this in an actual Nun's Catalogue. I checked the others' bras in the dormitory my freshman year. I'd run at odd times into that cavernous room and stolen looks at the underwear folded on the stools for the next day. B's and C's and 36's and 34's. I don't feel like a woman. I don't feel like a boy. I feel like some in between person. A Mary Martin-Peter Pan character. Every time I go to West End pool with Suzy I watch the girls on their old quilts talking to boys who are already smoking cigarettes. I can't help noticing the girls' perfect cleavages browning. I feel my face glow red with rage as I look at this miserable thing.

Catherine, on the other hand, is made like a movie queen. She, till she left for good one afternoon when I was at the pool, told me over and over that she is 36-23-36. I think I am 32-28-31. Not female, surely. But Catherine is pregnant and I am not, so that is one advantage to being the way I am.

I hear my father's light thud on the steps from the basement where his old painted and peeling desk sits as though it were something thrown away. He is a slender man, delicate and white; even he is sweating.

"Pack up." He says.

My mother stands the iron upright and switches it off. I think he doesn't see me packing right in front of his eyes.

"Dad, I am. There's my trunk. Here's my laundry."

"No," his says, "we're going away."

This news staggers me. We have never been away. How can seven people go anywhere? Where would they stay? But I don't ask any questions. Nor does my mother. We wake the girls, and I run to the field below for my brother. Within an hour we lock the house, get into the station wagon, no one arguing for windows. And then we're on our way, pulling out onto the highway to who knows where.

* * *

Beat up Cottages with one room and a powder room with little wrapped Camay soaps. Before we unpack, Charlie is down on the raft we rented for the day. He can't go in because he has just had an appendectomy we are still paying for. My father and mother seem to have lost their minds. They don't care that Charlie could fall in and break open his wound. They don't care that the girls are eating popsicles and it's dinnertime. My mother and my father set up three cots from the office, and I make them up. Our room is cool with the lake breezes blowing through the batiste at the windows. In one window, out the other. I stand at the open door too happy to breathe. Charlie, a small boat on the aqua wavelets. There's a lake in heaven I decide then and there.

* * *

The kids are so exhausted they willingly go to bed, Charlie in the full sized bed to sleep with my father, the girls on the cots. They look and smell wild, like animals, their hair in tufts, already bleached. My mother, father, and I sit just outside on the log at the edge of the waves to watch the sky change from peach, to orange, to greenish blue, to purple and finally to indigo. We've built a fire with driftwood and it blows tenderly.

Talking about things we never talk about, paintings and music, my brother in Viet Nam. We still don't talk about Catherine. My dad explains what it feels like to play the accordion and then talks to us a little about the stars, the constellations. They tell me the reason they let me stay up with them is that I'm a woman now. I'm grown up.

Suddenly I think: they are people; I never knew. I keep thinking that somehow it might be too late. For what I wonder?

I sleep with my mother, but a wind has come up and I roll over and over with the waves. My mother wakes, listens a moment and pats my hip. "Be still, Emmy, be still."

TWENTY SIX

WILLIAM JOHN

June, 1963

This is the third floor and sixty feet up. We are sitting on the sills, our legs inside, the rest of our body hanging outside doing the last window washing before the summer vacation. We wash the huge panes of glass with hot vinegar water and wipe them dry with old newspapers. I like how nothing goes to waste here, but think newspapers don't do the finest job.

If I fell out I would go splat like a bird. I would be a puddle of a person, all the liquids running out, the bones crushed like shells. I am amazed that I don't want that to happen. I want to get out of this place so I can pull some shorts over my skinny legs. I'm going to braid my hair and turn into an Indian even though I'm seventeen years old. I'll pack our waxed paper sandwiches and take my sisters and run right into the woods with them. The violets will be gone, but we can find Jack-in-the-Pulpits still. The creek. That's where we'll go. I told them to save their popsicle sticks so we can float them to the ocean. Then there's the Strawberry Festival that Suzy and I always go to. I'm going to get a peasant blouse and wear it off my shoulders. I remember how its Chinese Lanterns shake in the night breezes.

After today, two more days. After today, and two more days, my own bed, and trips to the bookmobile, and Schwartzle's Store for penny candy and cold pops slipped from crushed ice.

*   *   *

Dark. So still I can hear an old nun's wheezing. I am in the sacristy on the altar waiting for something. I don't know what. The tabernacle light flickers, a red heart on fire. It's my heart. I have a light in the dark of my own life. What is it? I pray to the baby who died, my unseen brother.

"William John. I know you're with God. I know you're right beside Him now. Help me."

Help me with what? Tomorrow I go home. Tomorrow a giant door whooshes open.

But I know something I don't have words for just now. It's as though William John dropped right out of heaven to kneel beside me. Someone taps my shoulder, but I can see no one.

"You can't be a saint, Emmy."

"But," I hiss at the voice. "Of course I can. Of course I can. Nothing's going to stop me."

"You can't be one here."

Silence. A stairway inside my chest. Going down, down, down. It's dark inside and outside my body. The old nun in the room next to the chapel makes a few choking sounds. I listen, thinking she might be dying in her sleep, but she returns to wheezing and I to my darkness.

"If I am not a saint, then I am nothing."

"You are a person," says the voice neither male nor female.

"A person for what? I don't want anything that exists in that world out there. I don't want a husband, I don't want a baby, and I don't want to have to try to make money; I'm too stupid. I will have no education. No college. I will be like my mother, chained and beaten."

"You are breaking, Emmy. You can feel yourself breaking."

Silence. Listening. Wanting not to listen.

"Imagine coming back next fall. How will you feel?"

Crazy. Worse than I am now. Magda gone for the new Convent down the mud road. I am looking into nothing. It grows blacker than the dark around me.

"You could be . . . Emmy."

"I can't imagine me as just a girl. What would I do? Work with my father in the basement? Write up orders for filthy rugs?"

Though it is June I rub my arms for warmth.

* * *

My trunk is in the hallway of the school by the double green doors. I am waiting for my mother to come for me. Most of the others are still packing. When I walk across the threshold to Sister Bernard's classroom I cannot believe what I am going to say. What am I going to say?

Sister is on her knees packing her books. I stare at her crucifix, just below my eyes. "Emmy," she says, rising. Smiling slightly. She doesn't want to but she likes me—no not "like," something else.

I stare at the floor.

"Emmy?"

I look up at her and shake my head. "I am not coming back."

Everything about her face changes. Her brows knit together. Her fine mouth twitches. Her nose grows wider and she leans her face into mine.

"Get your things. Leave me. Go!"

When my mother arrives, I extend my arms, but she brushes me aside, practical and rushed. She motions towards the trunk and between us we manage to pull and half carry the trunk to the station wagon. I kneel in the back and drag it in; then we go back for the rest of my things. When we have the last of it, and are about to open the doors, I hear Sister Bernard's voice.

"Mrs. Wilson. Mrs. Wilson."

Sister is running towards us as if we might escape. She has a small white envelope in her hand. Perhaps it is my grades, which I thought I would receive in the mail. She flips it without a word into my mother's hands. Before my mother can think, she opens the envelope and looks down. I look over her shoulder and see in elegant blue script, Sister Bernard's own hand, an itemized list with numbers and sums.

My mother's mouth is open and finally she asks, “What is it?”

Sister Bernard, her mouth drawn into a tight bow—does not respond at first. Then I can see her lips moving, but I do not understand the words.

"A bill, Mrs. Wilson. For Emmy's education."

*　　*　　*

When my mother turns the key in the ignition, and the motor wavers, then finally starts, I say, "Stop, stop, I forgot something." I jump out of the seat and rush, full speed, but my legs are stiff with fear and sorrow. When I get to my room I find it is still there, in my top drawer, my Maria Goretti prayer card. I grab it and place it in my bra as though I were stealing something. Flying down the staircase, I must be gone, but Sister Bernard slips from her classroom directly into my path. I pull back, terrified.

"Emmeline, you are turning your back on God; you are refusing his invitation." She waves her arm, her index finger pointing towards heaven.

“You will never be happy a single day in your life! Not a day!"

TWENTY SEVEN

THE STORY

October, 1963

Hushed talking. I am to introduce the play. The high school orchestra has not yet struck up. I am proud and embarrassed. My silly rabbit ears have been made by my mother and attached to a white angora headband. I'm in white tights and a huge white cardigan worn backwards, and I wear a pair of fluffy bedroom slippers. I've practiced hopping in front of my mother's bedroom mirror. Why couldn't I have been the witch or Gwendolyn? I fan the flames of my face, then stand riveted. Already they've begun to applaud. The music begins; I hop and spin onto the stage.

But the only thing I see is light.

AUTHOR'S NOTES

JCWatson has been writing from the age of twelve; her youthful success spurred her on to write poetry, short fiction, and novels since that time. She self-published her first volume of poetry in 2000. Following *Argument for Mercy,* she published a novel, *Current Wisdom,* by LBF Press in 2005 and in that same year two short fictions, *Reckless* and *The Flying Horse.* And in 2012, a poetry chapbook by Finishing Line Press, *The Journey of Lost Things. A Lake in Heaven* is a fictionalized memoir and her first novella.

She is currently working on a Chapbook, *The King of Bees* and a full length Poetry Manuscript, *The God of Pittsburgh,* and soon will have completed a collection of short stories, *Marcocito is Almost Dead.*

She was born in Pittsburgh, PA, the 3rd of seven children under the double yoke of a harsh Catholicism and hard scrabble poverty.

She has been a behavioral therapist for autistic children and an English Tutor and a classroom teacher for first generation Americans, including a program taught for Stanford University. She has also been a retailer, teachers' aide, nursery school teacher. And while attending Carnegie Mellon University, a cashier with the college's financial department.

JCW

CPSIA information can be obtained at www.ICGtesting.com
Printed in the USA
LVOW13s1727040514

384379LV00001B/40/P

9 780615 878478